GOLDEN MARE

GOLDEN MARE

MARE

WILLIAM CORBIN

Illustrated by Pers Crowell

Weekly Reader Books
Middletown, Connecticut

CONTENTS

CHAPTER

1

THE NEW ARRIVAL

THERE are a great many horses in the high country of the West, and some of them are lucky enough to have a boy to look after them and love them. But there aren't nearly enough boys to go around. That is why Magic, the golden mare, was most particularly lucky to have a boy like Robin Daveen.

It was the greatest kind of luck for both of them, as a matter of fact, that they had each other, because Magic was not an ordinary horse and Robin was not an ordinary boy.

Magic was a palomino with a mane like fresh pine shavings and a tail to match, and a way of looking out from under her long lashes that made a person think no horse could know so much or like so well the things it saw.

At least that's the way she looked to Robin, who knew her better than anyone else. That was the strange thing about Magic and Robin—no one but he could see her as she really was. Father couldn't, nor Mother. Certainly not Barry and Wynn, Robin's older brothers. Not even Old Clint, who worked for Father and smelled of snuff and was amazingly wise about almost everything else.

Robin would never forget the day he first found out about this peculiar blindness of theirs. It happened long ago—or so it seemed to him, now that he was twelve. It was the day Father brought home the new stallion—the big chocolate Tennessee walking horse with glaring eyes and a mane that fell in ripples to his shoulder. His name was Comet.

Wynn and Barry had dashed, whooping, from the house to watch while Father unloaded the new horse from the trailer and turned him into his corral. Robin, following slowly because he was not allowed to run, heard Father's deep voice saying proudly, "Take a good look, boys. It'll be a long time before you see another horse to equal him." The older boys had voiced their admiration loudly and then fallen into a heated argument over who should get to ride him first.

2

The New Arrival

The other horses—Sheila and Sunburst and Cotton and Dan—were plunging and milling in their corral, as excited as the boys. Behind them Robin could see Magic standing quietly in the open door of her box stall, her ears pricked forward in mild curiosity. He felt his usual thrill of pride as he looked at her.

Seeing Robin approach, Father called to him. "What do you think of him, boy? Isn't he a beauty?"

Robin had answered, saying what to him was quite obviously true, "He's all right, but he isn't half as pretty as Magic."

There was a moment of silence and then a shout of laughter that was like a slap in Robin's face. Wynn, who was four years older, hooted, "*That* old crowbait?" And Barry, who was only three years older but could hoot just as loud, said, "Father, you better get glasses for Robbie. He can't even tell a horse from a scarecrow!"

No one—Robin least of all—could have expected what happened next. Filled with a sudden, choking rage he bunched his fists and charged full tilt at Barry, who was nearest. He felt his blows land harmlessly as his brother backed away, heard his father's voice, loud with fright. Then the familiar, dizzying pain struck the middle of Robin's chest and he glimpsed Father's arms reaching toward him.

When he came to himself again he was in his bed and the doctor had been there. He could always tell because the doctor left a smell all his own. In the next room Mother was speaking quietly but her voice was fierce. "If you ever tease him about that horse again I swear I'll take a whip to both of you. You've been told a thousand times that it's dangerous to excite him or upset him. Now clear out of here, both of you, and don't let me catch sight of you till bedtime."

Surprisingly, Robin felt sorry for his brothers, for he was no longer angry. But at the same time he resolved he would never talk to them again, or to anyone else, of how he felt about Magic.

FRIENDS

THE promise Robin made that day was one that he kept a long time. He seldom thought about the reason for it. The real Magic was his secret to be shared with no one. He hardly remembered how Magic had come to mean as much to him as she did, though if he put his mind to it, a few things stood out above the mistiness of recollection like the tallest firs above a bank of fog.

For one, there was the first time he ever sat on Magic's back. It was Old Clint who had put him there, for Robin remembered the dusty-sharp smell of the old man's snuff and the thirsty-dry sound of his chuckle. And he remembered looking dizzily down from the horse's height, and the feeling that here he was no longer a very small boy whom everyone worried about and looked after. Here on this golden horse he was bigger than Barry, or Wynn, or Father even, bigger than anybody in the world—strong—unafraid. For her strength was his. The huge muscles that bunched and flowed and bunched again under her glossy hide were the muscles of Robin Daveen.

He could hear his own voice urging, "Fast, Clint, fast! Make her go fast!"

Then Old Clint's rough-edged voice. "Not this old girl. Her prancin' days is done." He patted the mare's side and his horny hand scraped Robin's leg. "Yep, she's a old lady now."

Robin spoke uneasily. "Is she as old as you?"

Clint gave his dusty chuckle. "Not in man-years, mebbe. But in horse-years I reckon she's a sight older'n me."

"But she—she'll get lots older, won't she?"

Clint must have heard the fear in Robin's voice, for he cocked his eye at the sun and reached in his overalls for the little round box of snuff—"Snoose," he always called it—and tucked a pinch of it behind his lower lip.

Because of these preparations Robin knew Old Clint was about to say something wise and deep, and he didn't want to miss a word of it.

When the old man had worked his jaw from side to side to settle the snoose comfortably, he spoke at last. "Now I've given that matter consider'ble thought, boy, and there's just no gettin' 'round it."

"What, Clint?"

"Fact is, I come to the conclusion that this here horse"—he poked a knobby finger into Magic's shoulder—"just plain ain't never goin' to die."

"How do you know?" Robin asked, relieved and yet afraid that for once the old man might be wrong.

Old Clint had laid a finger alongside his nose and looked down mysteriously and said, "There's ways of tellin', boy. Fact is, it's kind of a gift and there ain't many in the world has got it. Only knew one other man in all my days could do it besides me."

That settled it. Together they walked back to the house because it was suppertime and Robin said, "I'm glad she's always going to be here."

As they climbed the back porch steps the old man halted him and said, "One thing, boy. It wouldn't do to tell no one about this."

"Why not?" said Robin, puzzled and more than a little disappointed.

"Because," Clint answered, "if it was to get around how I can tell about horses and all, then ever'body in the country would be wantin' me to come and look at *their* horses and I wouldn't have no time to work for your pa. You see?"

"I see," Robin said, sighing. "Then I won't tell." And he never had.

That was the beginning of it.

When he grew a little older he was allowed to ride the golden mare by himself—but only after a family conference.

"It can't do him any harm," Father said. "She always was a steady one, and now she hasn't got spark enough to scare even a baby."

"Why must he ride at all?" asked Mother. "There are other things in this world to do besides ride around on horses."

"Every man should learn to sit a horse," Father said. "And shoot a rifle too. That's why I'm coaching the boy on shooting. And maybe later—" He didn't go on. It was always "maybe later" when people talked about Robin.

"All the same," Mother said, with her lips pressed straight, "he won't do it until we ask the doctor if it's all right."

So they asked the doctor, who cleared his throat and puffed out his cheeks in doctorly fashion, answering that he could foresee no ill effects —hurrack!—provided of course the proper caution were exercised—puffoo!—and the boy stayed strictly within the pasture—hurrack!—indulging in no antics such as racing about—puffoo!—and otherwise placing unneeded strain on—hurrack, hurrack!

No horse was ever mounted with more pride than the golden mare that day. Solemnly, like an astrologer of old performing some mysterious rite, Robin led her from her stall, across the corral to the gate that opened into the lower pasture. Her hoofs clopped softly on the bare ground of the corral, each step sending up a little puff of dust. She stood quietly while he climbed the gate and settled himself on her back, not without difficulty because he was carrying the new air rifle Father had given him. Magic turned her head and peered at him, an inquiring light in her great soft eyes, for it had been years since anyone had ridden her.

For a time he was content to sit astride her back, feeling her strength and sleekness, and to survey his new-found kingdom. The lower pasture sloped away before him to the east, bounded by the silver-green line of cottonwoods that hid the creek. Beyond the trees the ground sloped upward again until the green of the fields gave way to the bare brown hills where the upland range began. And beyond it all, at the very edge of the world, reared the monstrous bodies of the mountains, blue-white in the haze of summer.

The scent of clover hay was sweet in the high clear air. Father and Old Clint had cut and raked and baled it but hadn't yet picked it up to store in the vast barn loft. Still green, the bales lay scattered about in the field.

Robin's blue eyes moved from bale to bale and he smiled. Before him lay, not a thirty-acre stubble field dotted with bales of hay, but a boundless prairie across which moved a herd of buffalo. And Robin Daveen was a keen-eyed mountain man down from his upland meadows and his beaver streams, looking for fresh meat. He wore greasy buckskins, his hair was in braids like an Injun's and his powerful arms cradled a long Kentucky rifle.

Singling out the finest bull of them all, the mountain man kept his eye on it while he primed his rifle. Then he clicked with his tongue and clapped his heels against the ribs of his wiry Indian pony.

But nothing happened, and for a time the mountain man became a small boy astride a palomino who had carried hunters many times and now wanted only rest. She lowered her head and began to crop at the new grass coming up between the rows of stubble.

Robin spoke his first words to the golden mare then, the first of what were to be many thousands of words in the years ahead. He did it naturally, not even thinking about it, which without a doubt was the reason things turned out the way they did. Slinging the air rifle over his shoulder, he leaned forward across the hump of her withers until he was lying down, his arms circling as much of her neck as they could reach, and spoke quietly. "You have to go, Magic. Not for anyone

12

else. Only for me, because you're my horse now. You see?"

The snicking of Magic's teeth on the tender grass shoots stopped but her head did not come up. A long-tailed magpie flitted overhead. Robin could hear the beat of its wings but he did not look up.

Then slowly the mare raised her head and Robin's arms crept farther around her neck. Her ears twitched back.

"Now," said Robin, his voice no more than a whisper. "Now. Go now!" At the same time he squeezed his legs against her sides.

In a moment she sighed once—a small sound for so tremendous a body—and began to move. She went slowly at first, then faster—not much, but a little—turning right or left at the pressure of a knee, heading for the buffalo that was marked for slaughter. And the smile on the face of the mountain man was as bright as the sun.

The carcasses of bison lay thick on the plains that day and the deadly marksman was thinking of inviting all his Indian friends in for a feast, when a clatter of hoofbeats came along the lane that curved by the pasture on its way to the main road, half a mile away. The mighty hunter was so intent on drawing a bead on a final bull that he failed to hear the noise of cantering horses and the silence that followed when their riders drew rein and stared toward him.

What he couldn't fail to hear a moment later was Barry's voice, "Gee, look, a cowboy!"

The world of Robin's imagining shattered like a ball of glass, and he whirled to see the grinning faces of his brother and the older Alward boy from the next ranch north. Barry was on Cotton, a chestnut gelding. The Alward boy was on a leggy roan.

"A cowboy!" Barry whooped again. "A real, live cowboy, and he's shootin' Injuns!"

For a moment Robin could only stare.

"And did you see that horse go? Wow, ain't she a dinger? Look, like this!" Barry jabbed his heels into Cotton's flanks and hauled back on the reins.

Cotton reared, whirled and plunged off down the lane, dust smoking out behind him. "Bang!" yelled Barry. "Bang! Bang! Bang!" In a moment

he had whirled again and was coming back, crouched low in the saddle. "Bang! Another dead Injun! Bang-bang, another!"

At the point where the lane came nearest the pasture fence Cotton swerved, heading straight for the barbed wire, and for an instant Robin thought he was going to jump it. But Barry jerked the horse to a shuddering halt and grinned at his companion.

"Just like that he was going!" Barry said, "only faster. Ain't that right?" He was immensely pleased with himself.

"You bet," said the Alward boy. "He's a ridin', shootin' fool, that kid."

Then Barry's grin was gone, leaving fear in its place, for Robin had slid from the back of his horse, dropping the rifle, and had fallen to the stubble, picked himself up and started for the barn, running, stumbling, running again.

"Robbie! Robbie, don't run!" Barry shouted after him. "Wait, Robbie! I didn't mean anything. I was only playing. Please don't run!"

But for Robin the words were a meaningless jumble. He could think only of getting away from the sound of the voices and the sight of mocking eyes. The friendly, shadowy barn would shelter him.

He didn't remember that he should not run, until his bare feet felt the warm dust of the corral and pain stabbed into his laboring chest, but by then he didn't care.

The dusky coolness of Magic's stall welcomed him and he threw himself face down in the clean straw beneath the overhanging manger in the darkest corner, to wait for the pain. But perhaps because he really did not care, or because the other kind of pain was greater, it did not come and soon he found it easier to breathe.

Barry found him there. "Robbie!" he called breathlessly, pausing in the doorway. "Are you all right?"

Robin did not look up or answer. All he wanted was to be left alone.

The straw rustled as Barry crossed the stall and dropped to his knees beside the manger. There was fear in his voice and in the touch of his hand on Robin's shoulder. "You sick, Robbie? You got to tell me!"

"I'm not sick," said Robin. "Go away." He shrugged off his brother's hand.

Barry's voice was almost tearful with relief. "I didn't aim to be mean, Robbie. Honest. I was only kind of playing a game."

"Go away," said Robin.

"Don't be mad at me, Robbie. Here, I brought your gun."

"Go away!"

Barry got to his feet. "O.K., I'll go. But I'm sorry. Honest I'm sorry." At the door he turned, looking back at his brother. "You *really* sure you're all right?"

But no sound came from the small figure in the corner of the stall and Barry went away, kicking at the dust of the corral.

For a long time Robin lay thinking, remembering, and wishing he had never learned to think or to remember. Surely the world had never been so cruel and lonely until Robin Daveen came into it.

His thoughts had reached their bitterest depth when his ears caught the thud of slow, patient hoofs in the corral outside, and he rolled over on his back, staring in surprise as the figure of the mare loomed in the doorway, cutting off the glare of the sun outside. Robin lay very still.

For a moment she paused there, half in

shadow, half in sunlight, her nostrils moving as she sought out the unfamiliar scent among the familiar, her gentle eyes peering toward him in the gloom.

"Magic!" Robin whispered. And the golden mare stepped toward him, her head came down, her velvety nose brushed his arm and she nudged him, rolling him half over in the straw as though he was no more than a straw himself. All at once Robin was laughing. He scrambled to his feet and reached up high enough almost to encircle her neck with his arms. She drew cautiously back for fear she might tread on him, and stood patiently while his fingers twined among the tassels of her mane. A sound that was like a gentle wind blew up from her massive chest and tickled Robin warmly on the neck. He laughed again and the world was no longer a lonely place.

3

OLD CLINT CONFESSES

ROBIN decided the very next day that he alone should feed the golden mare. Or rather he must have decided during the night while he slept because his first thought when he woke was, "Today I will tend to feeding Magic. Today and tomorrow and all the days after."

It was not hard to arrange because Wynn, whose job it was to feed all the horses twice a day, was glad to be rid of Magic, who meant extra work for him. Her box stall was separated by the width of the barn from the row of tie stalls where the other horses spent the nights. He could drop hay from the loft directly into the mangers of the others but hay for Magic had to be carried along a corridor past the feed bins and the tack room. This added about two minutes to Wynn's labors and he was always in a hurry. Robin had heard him grumble about it more than once.

"You mean you *want* to?" he said when Robin followed him to the barn and brought the matter up. "But what if you'd forget?" he added after a moment, remembering that his responsibilities as the oldest brother were majestically important.

Robin solemnly assured him that he would rather forget his own breakfast and supper than Magic's.

"Tell you what, then," said Wynn. "Whenever I feed the rest of them I'll throw down a couple slabs of hay for her, right where you're standing there, and you can pick 'em up. You know where the oats are. Give her that coffee can full, morning and night. No more'n that, though, she's fat enough already."

"She isn't either fat," said Robin, but he said it under his breath. There was no use getting into an argument with Wynn.

With a slab of hay under each arm, Robin marched past the feed bins. He couldn't carry the can of oats too. Hearing his footsteps, Magic nickered eagerly from behind her high divided door. Robin slipped the catch on the lower half of the door and ducked under the top. When he tossed the hay into the manger she sniffed at it, nudged it with her nose a time or two, then turned her head and looked at him reproachfully. Robin laughed. "All right, I'll get the oats, but you're really not supposed to eat dessert till last."

When he brought the oats and dumped them in a corner of the manger, she attacked them with such obvious satisfaction that Robin laughed again and said, "If they're that good I'll always bring them first."

That was exactly what he did until the time came when he was big enough to carry both oats and hay at once.

As the weeks went by, and the months, Robin spent more time with the golden mare. He was not allowed to go to school like his brothers, or to play the games they played. Someday, perhaps, he might go to school, the doctor said—one could never tell about this particular type of rheumatic fever. But Robin knew that day would be long in coming, and he was content to study the lessons Mother gave him and to spend long hours with Magic.

Perching on the edge of her manger, or lying in the straw beneath it, where he could look through the open door, across the lower pasture to the creek and to the green-brown hills and white mountains beyond, he talked to her endlessly. He repeated to her the lessons he had learned and it helped him learn them better. And then he would tell her the stories he had read in his books—of the great King Arthur and the noble knights who roamed the countryside seeking wrongs to right and monsters to slay and damsels to defend; of the ancient heroes who sailed the seas to find the golden fleece, or slay the dreaded Gorgons, or lop off the heads of tyrant kings; of wars and marches and battles, of Indians and scouts, of saints and sailor men, and the bloody doings of buccaneers.

And then as time went on he began to tell a new kind of story, the kind that came drifting into his head out of nowhere: stories of the great white bears of the mountaintops who came out of their lairs only when the snow was swirling down and the wind was awake, and so were never seen by man; stories of the little folk who lived in the heart of the mountain and never came out at all; stories of animals and people and places whose like had never been seen on the earth.

The golden mare could chew and chop away

at her hay with the teeth that were left her, swish her long white tail, or merely stand peering dreamily out into the far distance, the same as Robin. But now and then she would turn her head and nibble at his arm or cheek just to show that she was listening. Her breath was warm and smelled of the sweet hay.

During this time a strange thing happened— though it didn't seem strange at the time. Like growing taller, it happened so gradually Robin was not even aware of it. Day by day the golden mare grew more beautiful, her coat more glossy, her mane and tail more silkily glistening, her step more graceful, and her eyes more luminous. It is true that Robin brushed her every day with the stiff wire brush from the tack room, combed her mane and tail and the long forelock between her eyes, and oiled her hoofs until they gleamed. But these things would not account for the way she moved, for the way she held her head proud-arched. To Robin, though, they needed no accounting for; they existed, he could see them regardless of what anyone else could see, and that was good enough for him.

He, of course, didn't know how she looked to

others, for he never thought about it. Nor did he know that Old Clint, working around the barn, would sometimes come close to the stall's partition and listen, one gnarled hand cupped to his ear, a look of wonder on his face. Neither would he see that look return when the old man told Father what he had heard.

"Beats me how he's learnt so many things, that young'un," he said on one such occasion. "Reckon he knows twice't as much as the other two put together. He tells that ol' horse about things and places I never even heard of, and talks with words I can't pernounce, let alone know what they mean."

Father put his paper down and with a frown pulled off the glasses he used for reading. "Books!" he rumbled. "That's where he learns it all. Every time I go to town I have to bring back half the library with me. I swear I don't know what the boy will come to—grow up without knowing real from make-believe, probably."

That was the signal for Mother to put aside her sewing or her darning, a gentle fire in her eyes. "You're a good one to talk about make-believe! A man who always spends half his time play-

ing cowboy instead of settling down to work!"

"Changing the subject!" Father snorted. "Just like a woman."

"All right, then, I'll go back to it! Just tell me what's wrong with reading and learning. Seems to me we could do with a little more of both around here. And what's wrong with make-believe? Maybe he'll grow up"—her dark eyes grew dreamy—"to be a great playwright, or a novelist."

"Maybe so, maybe so," said Father. "All the same I wish he was well. I wish he could do things like the other boys."

It was a mistake and Father should have known better, for it only brought a new outburst from Mother. "Why has he got to be like other boys? Why do men always think every boy ought to be just like every other boy? It would be a silly world, wouldn't it, if they all grew up to be bronco busters—or ballplayers!"

Father threw up his hands in mock surrender. "All right, I know when I'm licked." He winked at Old Clint. "It's all your fault, you got her started." He got up and patted Mother on the shoulder. "It's all right. I'll let the boy be what he wants.

He's going to anyway. And he'll be the best—he's too much like you to be anything else."

Not many weeks later another conversation took place that would have interested Robin and disturbed him too if he had heard it.

Father and Old Clint had been harvesting oats in the north field, for it was late summer. They had sat down in the shade of the monstrous red grain combine for a breather and a smoke. Father, at any rate, had a smoke while the old man slipped a charge of snoose under his lip and cleared his throat resoundingly, for there was something on his mind.

"Been thinkin'," he began abruptly, " 'bout a thing I done that was wrong."

"What you been up to, Clint," said Father, puffing on his pipe, "sheep stealing?"

"Ain't no joke," said Old Clint with dignity. "It's got to do with that boy of yours."

"Robin?" asked Father, knowing there couldn't be anything about the older boys to put a wrinkle in the old man's brow.

"Somethin' I told him a long time back, somethin' I'd plumb forgot till yesterday when I seen

29

the boy a-headin' fer the old mare's stall with his book under his arm like always, and her a-lookin' through the c'ral fence, watchin' him come."

"Yes, I know," said Father. "What about it?"

Old Clint ignored the interruption. "Occurred to me to wonder, with the mare so old and all, what's goin' to happen to the boy when she dies?"

"We'll worry about that when it happens," Father snapped. The painful thought had occurred to him already. "The boy will have to face up to it, that's all."

"But what I done," pursued the old man, "was to make it worse. He'll never believe a word I say again."

"What in Sam Hill you driving at, Clint? Get on with it!"

Old Clint spat and wiped his mouth with the back of his hand to prove he wouldn't be rushed. "It's what I recollected yesterday. I told him, back when he was a tiny shaver, that that ol' horse wasn't never goin' to die!"

"You what?"

Clint nodded. "My very words. I up and said she'd live forever, that I had a way of knowin'."

"Well, if you aren't a thundering old idiot!"

"Worse'n that," said the old man. "Seemed all right at the time. I was just cheerin' him up like, thinkin' he'd fergit about it, same as I done. But knowin' that boy like I know him now I'd bet a month's pay he ain't fergot a word of it."

"All I can say," said Father, knocking his pipe against the combine's massive wheel, "is you'd better have another story ready when the time comes. And it better be a jim-dandy!"

THE BIG SNOW

THE winter of that year—Robin's tenth—was one which he and nobody else would ever forget. It was the winter of the Big Snow.

The high country was no stranger to snow and wind and bitter cold, but not even in the memory of Old Clint had there been a winter like the one of the Big Snow. It came early, trampling on the heels of autumn. The radio said solemn things about arctic air masses and low-pressure areas, and Father scanned the western skies and said, "There's weather making up, all right. We're in for an early winter." Then he saw the nearly empty wood box on the back porch and called for Barry and Wynn. "There'll be no play for the two of you," he said, "until that box is full. And I mean heaped up till it won't heap any more."

"Aw, can't we do it later?" pleaded Wynn. "We were going up to—"

"You heard what I said," Father told him, but he smiled at the boy who looked so much like himself and added, "Trouble with you is 'later' means the same as 'not at all.' Clint, if you get time, hook up the 'dozer blade to the cat. Got a notion we might be needing to move some snow."

Robin, feeling excitement in the air and wishing that, just once, he could be a part of things, stood by the great woodpile behind the pump house and watched his brothers swing their axes lackadaisically, splitting the upended logs into kindling for the kitchen stove. Ambling behind him came old Mac, the Airedale whose graying coat, growing thin in spots, no longer concealed the scars of savage battles with mountain lions he had trailed and cornered. The dog peered around him idly for a moment and then flopped down on the grass with a grunt and a sigh as though he hadn't really expected to see anything of interest. Without knowing it Robin sighed too, so forcefully that Wynn grinned at him unexpectedly and said, "What's the matter, Robbie? It make you tired just looking at us hard-working characters?"

Pleased and faintly surprised as always by attention from his older brother, Robin smiled back at him. "I was just wishing," he said, "that I could chop a little."

"Well—I don't know—" began Wynn doubtfully.

"Here," put in Barry, a mischievous gleam in his eye, "take my ax."

Robin looked at Wynn. "Do you suppose it's all right?"

"Just for a minute—one log, maybe," Wynn said.

Robin's hands closed comfortably around the hickory handle, satin-smooth from long use. He raised the gleaming blade above his head, gauged the distance carefully and let fly. Thwump! Missing the log completely the axhead buried itself in the ground and Robin glanced quickly at his brothers, looking for a sign of ridicule. There wasn't the ghost of a smile on either face.

"It's the way you were standing," said Barry hurriedly. "You got to plant your feet far apart. Here, like this."

"He was standing all right," put in Wynn. "It's the way you hold your hands, Robbie. Let your right hand slide up on the upswing and then back down when you take your cut. Watch how I do it."

"Watch nothing!" exploded Barry. "All Robbie could learn watching you is how to cut off a leg."

"Big talk!" said Wynn with a superior smile. "I can outchop you any day in the week including Easter and the Fourth of July!"

Robin, who could see that his wood-chopping lesson was getting nowhere, had a sudden idea—a keeping-the-peace idea. "Why don't you have a contest?" he suggested.

"Why not?" said Wynn.

"Any time!" Barry said.

"Here's how you could do it," Robin said eagerly. "Each of you take so many logs—ten maybe—and split each one into four pieces. First one to get through is the winner."

"Good idea," approved Wynn. "Only make it twenty. Endurance ought to count for something."

Barry said, "Make it a hundred, for all I care."

"Twenty ought to be enough," put in Robin. "I'll give the signal to start."

"O.K.," said Wynn. "And we pick our own logs, so neither of us can say he lost because his logs were knottier or something."

Robin helped set up logs in rows of twenty. Barry and Wynn took their places, each at the end of his row, while Robin stationed himself where he could watch without being in the way.

"When I say 'three'," he called out in a louder voice than was really necessary, "you can start. All ready? One—two—THREE!"

The axes fell in twin arcs and the crack of the splitting wood was like a single pistol shot. Robin felt as excited as though he were a contestant rather than a spectator. He could hardly keep from cheering.

The ax blows cracked in a ragged rhythm, punctuated by the grunts of the boys as they strained at their work, with now and then an exclamation of annoyance when a log, split once and too hastily set up for the next blow, toppled over before the ax could strike. Barry moved ahead from the start, and was attacking his seventh log by the time Wynn finished his fifth.

Robin's imagination quickly convinced him

that he, not his brothers, was in control of the flashing axes. Wynn was his right hand, Barry was his left. Merely by tightening one fist he could speed the action on one side, or by loosening the fist he could slow it. First he would give Barry a commanding lead, then slowly bring Wynn up from behind and end the contest in a tie with a whirlwind finish. Robin's left fist tightened and Barry forged ahead. Three logs—four logs—five logs—until by the thirteenth log he was ahead by four. His face was streaked with sweat and he was gasping for breath.

Now was the time. Robin squeezed his right hand and loosened his left a trifle. Barry's ax slipped in his hands and glanced off the fourteenth log. He grunted angrily and stooped to set it up again. Wynn's ax rose and fell with the tirelessness of a machine. He gained one log, then another. The gap was closing fast and Robin, watching every movement, was so carried away by the strange power he was wielding that he failed to hear a step behind him. He jumped when a scratchy chuckle sounded in his ear. Old Clint, spitting carefully to one side, observed,

"The tortoise and the hare all over again, hey?"

Robin bumped dismally back to reality. Wynn was catching up, of course, because he had saved his wind and strength, not because Robin's fist had tightened, but Robin couldn't help resenting Clint's interruption. "It's going to be a tie," he said.

"Wouldn't risk no money on it," Clint replied. He chuckled again. "Whichever'n wins, it's a sight to look at. Never knowed them two could hustle so."

Both Robin and the old man were right. Both boys put on a burst of speed, but Barry pushed his strength too far and when his last half log lay split in two he whirled to find his brother waiting, his axhead resting on the ground.

By the bitterness of the disappointment in his brother's face Robin saw how much Barry had wanted—even needed—to win. Glancing quickly at Wynn's dark, sweat-streaked face, Robin knew by a subtle change in the look of triumph there that Wynn too had caught that flash of bitterness. There was a pause broken only by the sound of labored breathing.

Barry was the first to speak. Dropping his ax and rubbing his hands on his jeans, he found the courage for a weak grin. "You can't say," he panted, "I didn't give you—a run for your money."

Robin saw Wynn's black brows bunch in a scowl over his bold eyes. He was like Father. Whatever he felt strongly inside always managed to look like anger when it got as far as his face. Now he blurted, "Run for my money, nothing—you won!"

Barry stared. "What you talking about? You got done first, didn't you?"

"Sure I did," said Wynn, scowling more fiercely than ever. "But I fouled one up, back towards the middle. Only cut it in three sticks instead of four. Thought I'd have time to go back and finish it, but I didn't."

"Where's the one you fouled up?" Barry's voice was skeptical yet eager.

Robin glanced along Wynn's line of split logs. They lay scattered in all directions. There would be no way to tell which log had been improperly split.

"Robbie, count 'em," commanded Wynn.

"You're the judge. If my row's only got seventy-nine sticks instead of eighty, Barry wins."

"Count mine first," demanded Barry excitedly.

Robin was happy to be at the center of things again. While the others watched he counted quickly but carefully, saying each number under his breath so as not to forget. Reaching the end of Barry's row he straightened and turned.

"Well," came Barry's impatient voice, "there's eighty, aren't there?"

"Eighty exactly," said Robin solemnly and bent again to his task.

The other row, too, held exactly eighty sticks and Robin knew he had not miscounted.

"How many, how many?" called Barry from his seat on the woodpile.

Robin looked almost shyly, not at Barry, but at Wynn and the black scowl that hid his secret kindness. He spoke softly. "Just like Wynn said, there's seventy-nine."

"Wow!" Barry leaped to his feet, forgetting he was tired, snatched up his ax and brandished it over his head. "You hear that, Clint? You hear who's the champeen woodchopper?"

Age had not dulled the old man's eyes and ears. "I reckon," he said dryly, "you ought to do the whole job all the time, now you know you're so handy at it."

But Barry wasn't listening. Full of his victory, he gave a warwhoop and flipped his ax high in the air, end over end. Catching it neatly by the handle he flashed a look at Old Clint, seeking approbation. But the old man's voice was dryer than ever. "That was the durndest-fool stunt I seen in many a day. Time you learnt a little sense, boy."

"Come on, Flash," Wynn said sarcastically, "let's get this wood into the house while you still got two hands."

"Leave it to the champ, Wynn," put in Old Clint. "Your pa sent me to say he could use you a while down at the machine shed."

Robin watched regretfully as Wynn walked off with Old Clint. Then he eyed Barry without much hope and said, "Maybe now you could show me what you started to—you know, about chopping?"

But Barry had lost his teaching enthusiasm along with his audience. "Well," he began hesitantly, "I'll do it some other time. Right now I got all this wood to carry in, and then I—I promised Walt Hansen I'd come over today and—" He began to load his arm with the sticks of wood.

For a moment Robin was tempted to tell him he hadn't really won the chopping contest. But he didn't and, after Barry staggered off toward the house with twice the load he should have carried, Robin leaned down and rubbed the wiry fur of old Mac, who lay sleeping at his feet. "I suppose you're busy too," he said. The old warrior signified he was by opening one eye briefly, twitching his stump of a tail just once and promptly going back to sleep.

Robin sighed and stood up. He looked at the two axes gleaming dully on the ground and thought how fine it would be if he were allowed to chop all day long without ever stopping. Loneliness closed over him like the chill in the air and after a while he wandered off toward the barn and the golden mare.

She was stretched out comfortably in the straw when he came, but she nickered a greeting and made no complaint when he sat on her back and thrust his hands under her mane to warm them.

"No lessons today, Magic," he said. "We got them all done yesterday, and this is Saturday."

Her ears twitched back, then forward again, and she blew gently through her nose, a companionable sound, and Robin fell to staring out the door across the pasture and the creek where the leafless cottonwoods stirred restlessly. A line of crows, flying low, passed overhead. The upland range, already gray with winter, stretched up and out and on forever, for the mountains beyond were drowned in a slate-hued sea of cloud.

Robin shivered and buried his hands deeper in Magic's silvery mane. "Winter's coming early and it's going to snow," he said, still thinking of the invisible mountains. "Up there I guess it's already coming down fast—and the wind is heaping it up in drifts as high as houses—higher than palaces even, and cathedrals."

He was silent while the pictures came up in his mind, dissolved and made way for other pictures, and then the words came.

"You remember, Magic—you remember what

it's like because of the time we were there, you and I. The time Father came home and told of shooting an elk and wounding it, and how it bounded away behind Castle Rock and he never saw it again. Remember? And we waited till dark because we knew they wouldn't let us go and we slipped away and I rode you to Castle Rock and picked up the trail by moonlight. I had my rifle, remember—not to kill the elk for fun but because we knew we couldn't let him go on wounded and suffering.

"All that night and all the next day we followed the trail, up to the timber line and on, and it was steep and rocky and we had nothing to eat. But you never faltered or stumbled. And then the storm came—wild and cold with the snow piling up—just the way it's doing now. . . ."

It was a story like other stories, so real to Robin that he scarcely knew where story left off and real life took hold again, and time meant nothing either to him or to Magic, for the sun slid westward on an unseen course beyond the rock-gray sky. Once in the middle of the tale the golden mare grew hungry and heaved to her feet while Robin, clinging fast to her back, talked on.

But things-as-they-are intruded at last and Robin woke to the fact that he was growing cold. The wind was on the prowl and the open door of the stall, held back against the side of the barn by a length of wire, was rattling and banging, almost breaking free. It could have been three o'clock in the afternoon, or perhaps five.

Sliding from Magic's back, Robin hurried to unhook the wire and wrestle the big door shut against the pull of the wind. Then he said a quick good night to the mare and headed for the house with his chin tucked low, remembering of course that he must not run. As he reached the steps to the back porch the first touch of snow, hard and sharp like grains of sand in the driving wind, peppered his cheek and made his eyes squint up.

Supper that night was a jumpy time because Father kept muttering to himself and shoving his chair back to stride to the shelf where the barometer stood. He would peer at it and shake his head, then turn to the window and stare out, cupping his hands around his eyes to cut out the light of the room. Then he would sit down to the table

45

again and spear a piece of meat with his fork as though it were an enemy.

The others tried to look as though they noticed nothing unusual, but even Mother could not conceal an occasional start when the wind, whooping down from north of west, would hold itself in for a moment or two and then let go with a slap like a hand of a careless giant and set the house to shuddering. Only Old Clint ate on undisturbed, his store teeth clicking. "Set down, Bob," he said when Father made his third trip to the barometer and the window. "It ain't nothing but a old-time blizzard out of Canada. Blow itself out by mornin'."

Morning came, though, and the wind roared on with the snow in its teeth. Robin heard it the moment he woke and he sat up suddenly, the movement sucking chill air up between the bedclothes and his body. The powder-fine snow came hissing against his window. The window itself, when he got up to look, was like a huge blind eye, for there was nothing to be seen through it but the gray-white of the storm. Even the sycamore tree on the lawn outside was invisible.

Snatching his clothes, Robin hurried downstairs to dress by the kitchen fire. Father and Old Clint, who had already eaten, were stuffing themselves into heavy sheepskin coats, encumbered by wool shirts and sweaters underneath. Clint wound a woolen scarf around his face and head until only his eyes and his bony nose were showing.

"Seventeen below," he said, his voice a muffled squeak from behind the layers of wool, "and still a-goin' down. This here's a real ring-tailed ripsnorter."

Father turned down the earflaps of his stained old hunting cap and jammed it on his head. "Let's go," he said. "It's already drifted belly-deep to a tall Injun between here and the barn."

While Robin ate his buckwheat cakes he heard the sound, now loud, now muffled by the wind's roar, of the caterpillar tractor as it labored to clear a path from the barn to the other buildings, then to the house and down the lane to the highway.

Finishing his breakfast, Robin bundled up in his warmest clothes, including the sheepskin coat

that had been Barry's the winter before and which was still a little too big for Robin. He was shrugging into it when Mother looked up from the slab of bacon she was slicing and asked in surprise, "Where in the world are you going?"

"To feed Magic," he replied.

"Oh, not this morning! There's no use your going out in a storm like this. Let Wynn tend to her when he feeds the others."

"It won't hurt me," Robin said quickly, "and I'll only stay a little while." Then he slipped out the door before she could protest further.

Outside, the wind's fury struck him like the blow of an ax and spun him halfway round. The driving snow seared his cheek and he stumbled down the steps, nearly falling until he could manage to brace himself against the blast. Between the house and barn he met Old Clint, hurrying in with a foaming bucket of milk in each hand. A huge drop glistened on the tip of the old man's nose and tears of cold were running down his leathery cheeks. He shouted something above the noise of the wind, but Robin hurried on to the shelter of the barn.

The horses in their line of stalls nickered eagerly. Cotton, the big chestnut, rolled his milky eye and pawed at the floor. Ignoring them all, Robin filled his oat can and went on to Magic's stall.

Twin jets of steam poured from her nostrils into the icy air as she gave him her usual greeting, and he watched with satisfaction as she licked up the oats from the smooth boards of the manger. While she ate he stroked her neck and talked about the storm. Then, struck by a sudden thought, he went back to the tack room and with some difficulty pulled down a padded horse blanket from the nail it hung on.

Throwing the heavy blanket over the high back of the golden mare wasn't easy but on the fourth attempt Robin achieved it. Fastening the stubborn buckles underneath her belly was even harder because he had to take off his mittens to do it and his fingers quickly grew numb. But after warming them several times against her flank he succeeded in fastening the blanket, and stood back to view the result.

"There," he told her, "now you won't care how cold it gets."

It had been a long time since anyone had taken the trouble to provide Magic with a blanket. She shook herself experimentally to see if the strange garment would come off. It didn't and she gazed with mild reproof at Robin, who had broken into sudden laughter.

Just then, above the noise of the wind outside, Robin heard the thunder of the big cat's motor and the clatter-clank of its treads. Then a door banged at the far end of the barn.

Leaving Magic's stall, Robin found Father stamping his feet and blowing on his hands. The horses, stretching their necks toward him as far as their halter ropes would go, were stamping and calling hungrily. Father frowned and muttered something under his breath. When he caught sight of Robin coming from the tack room, his frown deepened. "Oh, it's you," he said. "Where's Wynn?"

"I don't know," Robin replied, and Father said, "Well, get up to the house and tell him I said to come out here pronto and feed these horses. I've got enough on my hands without doing his work for him."

Wynn was eating his breakfast when Robin gave him the message. "You better hurry," he added. "He seems awful mad about something."

His brother made no reply but he stuffed an enormous forkful of pancakes into his mouth, got up and reached for the sweater and coat that lay in a heap on a chair where he had left them. In a moment he was gone, the kitchen door slamming thunderously.

Robin, getting out of his coat and mittens, saw Mother pick up Wynn's plate with a sigh and take it to the sink. After a moment he asked, "Is it the cattle Father's worried about mostly?"

"Yes," Mother said. "You know they're up on the range."

"Will they freeze to death?" asked Robin, round-eyed, feeling suddenly guilty that he hadn't even given a thought to the cattle wandering among the blizzard-swept hills.

"Nah, they won't freeze," put in Barry, talking with his mouth full. "They know enough to get behind some rocks or something and huddle together to keep warm."

"That's right," said Mother patiently, "but the

snow will cover the grass. They'll have nothing to eat."

"We'll go get 'em!" said Barry, to whom everything seemed easy until he started out to do it. "We'll drive 'em down to the pasture."

"In this storm?" Mother said. "You couldn't even find them."

"Well, when the snow stops. We'll find them then."

"*If* it stops," said Mother. "But it's shown no sign of it yet, and the weatherman says a new storm is on the way. The drifts could get so deep there'd be no way to get the cattle out even if they were found."

"Then—then they'll starve to death?" Robin burst out.

Mother smiled. "We won't worry about that now. The things we fear the most don't often happen to us. Why don't you get a towel, Robin, and dry these dishes for me?"

Robin dried the dishes, but the wind roared on outside and every time a sudden gust hammered at the house he shivered, thinking of the cattle. In his mind he saw them crowded for days and days in the lee of some rocky ledge while the icy blast howled around them and their sides grew gaunt with hunger.

STORMBOUND

ALL that day and night, and for another day and night as well, the blizzard raged, burying the high country ever deeper in snow. On the second night the telephone went dead when a pole blew down somewhere along the line, and on the evening of the following day the electric power went off. The lack of light was not the worst of it, for there were kerosene lanterns for the barn and candles for the house, but soon there was no water to cook with, to wash in, or even to drink, because the pump that drew water from the well was powered by electricity. The radio was a silent, useless box of tubes and wires. The family were prisoners of the storm, cut off from the rest of the world so completely that it seemed to Robin there was no one else alive upon the planet.

There was no way of knowing whether it might

be hours or days or even weeks before the power would be restored. Father and Old Clint, working in the bitter cold of the pump house, labored through the night and far into the following day to rig up a gasoline engine that would drive the pump.

At intervals they warmed up the cat and cleared new paths through the ever drifting snow. Each morning Robin, in spite of Mother's protests, heated a pail of water on the kitchen stove and carried it out to melt the ice that covered Magic's water tub.

As the stormy hours passed, Father's temper grew shorter and he wore a frown of worry constantly. Then, sometime during the small hours of the fourth night, the wind eased and the snow stopped falling.

Robin was aware of it the instant he woke, just before dawn, to the sound of Father's boots as he kicked them free of snow on the back steps.

The wind had been pounding and the snow hissing for so long that the silence now was like a noise and Robin had the curious feeling that he had been deaf for a long time and only now regained his hearing. From the kitchen below came the faint clatter of silverware and dishes, and the dull, metallic thump of stove lids. Mother was already up and making breakfast. Robin hurled the covers off, snatched his clothes from a chair and sped down the stairs to the warmth of the kitchen fire.

Father was just sitting down to the table and Mother was piling eggs and bacon and fried potatoes on his plate. His face was bright red from the cold, but his frown was gone and he smiled when he caught sight of Robin. "Well!" he boomed. "At least we've got one early bird in the litter. Are those lazy louts still pounding their ears?"

"Shall I wake them?" Robin offered, feeling good inside because Father was cheerful again.

"Do that, will you, boy?" asked Father. "They can saddle up for me while I'm finishing breakfast."

"I'll have your coffee in a minute," said Mother from the stove. This time, Robin noticed with surprise, it was she who was frowning. In a moment she added, "Are you dead set on going up there in this awful cold? It's nearly thirty below, Clint told me. Can't you at least wait?"

"Wait for what?" said Father, talking around a mouthful of potatoes. "Wait for the cattle to die and then go hunt for their bones? For all we know there may be more snow coming and then it'll be too late. No, I've got to go now. The least I can do is find them while the weather's clear. Then I'll know what can or can't be done."

"Are you going to ride up there," Robin asked, "in all those snowdrifts?"

"I'd fly, Robbie," said Father, winking at him, "but my wings are busted. If horses can't get through, nothing can. Now you run upstairs and rout out those boys."

At first Wynn and Barry told him sleepily to go away and leave them alone, but when he told them Father was getting ready to ride to the upland range they bounded out of bed, grabbing for their clothes.

When Robin came back to the kitchen, both his brothers were talking at once and Father had to slap the table with a heavy hand to quiet them. "Neither of you is going anywhere this morning," he said in a voice that couldn't be argued with. "This is no job for a boy." A smile eased the sternness of his tone. "But there'll be plenty to do later on. Right now get out there and saddle Comet and Sheila. They're the toughest of the lot. Put a lead rope on Sheila and give them both double rations of oats. Oh yes, and rig the rifle boot to Comet's saddle. And one other thing—"

Father broke off, listening intently, for there was an unexpected interruption. Old Mac, who slept beside the stove near the wood box, had scrambled suddenly to his feet and loosed a long-drawn, unearthly sound that was somewhere between a whine and a howl.

"What's the matter with—" Barry began, but Father silenced him with a gesture and listened, one ear cocked toward the door.

For a moment there was silence except for the hiss of burning pinewood in the stove. And then it came—from what direction Robin couldn't tell, nor from what distance, for it could have been within the very house itself, or miles away. At first it was a sweet, haunting sound, like a high note of a violin; then it plunged down the scale until it was an ugly shouted threat that made the back of Robin's neck turn cold. The old dog went to Father, clicking along the floor with claws overgrown from long disuse. He nudged Father's knee, whining deep in his throat and turning his grizzled muzzle toward the door, pleading to be let loose.

Father rumpled the dog's curly gray hair and muttered, "Your day is over, old scout. Take it easy." To the others he said, "Cougar. I'm not surprised. The storm's driven them out of the mountains and they're hungry for meat. They're smart devils when they're starving. We'll have to keep an eye out."

"Bet I could nail the varmint," Barry said, "if he came too close."

"O.K., Dan'l Boone," said Father, grinning, "let's see you get one between here and the barn. Go saddle me those horses, you two, because you won't eat till you do."

After a brief but strenuous battle with Comet, who was bent on going back to the barn rather than face the cold trail, Father got away soon after daybreak. The patient Sheila, laden with blankets, firewood, food and hot coffee, followed behind at the end of her lead rope.

Robin and the others watched him ride down to the frozen creek and disappear along its bank, then reappear a few minutes later on the slope beyond. Even at that distance they could see the horses struggle and flounder belly-deep in the drifts.

"Up yonder," Old Clint observed, "he'll stick to the ridges, where the snow's thin." Then he added, "Glad it's him instead of me. That there ain't no joy ride he's a-goin' on."

The day dragged endlessly for all of them. Even Robin, who was used to amusing himself in quiet ways, found it hard to pass the time. He

paid two visits to Magic but each time the bitter cold soon drove him back to the warmth of the kitchen. Mother, mainly to keep the older boys occupied, set all three of them to work cleaning house. For a while it was fun. Wynn and Barry clowned their way through the sweeping and dusting, pretending to be the English housemaids they had once heard on a radio program. They addressed each other as Agatha and Gertrude, speaking in high falsetto voices with what they imagined to be British accents. Robin encouraged them with his laughter but at last they tired of the game and grew irritable and argumentative.

In the afternoon they invited him to join them in a target shooting match, using Father's .22. Though Robin could not go hunting with the others, Father had taught him to shoot and he was nearly as good a marksman as his brothers. They shot tin cans off a fence post until their fingers, stiff with cold even in gloves, could no longer squeeze the trigger.

The long afternoon came to an end at last, the wintry twilight lingered for a while and then it was full night.

TO THE RESCUE

MOTHER had reluctantly given up waiting dinner. She had also given up peering out the window at intervals toward the northeast and the upland range. She said very little and was cheerful as always, but still, Robin noticed, there was something—a kind of absent-mindedness—to show she was worried.

The boys, and Old Clint with them, had feasted on lean short ribs of beef, and mashed potatoes and peas and squash and gooseberry pie. The old man was reaching for his after-dinner snooze when the call came—a long, low muffled "Hallooooo" from somewhere down by the creek.

Everyone rushed for the door, catching up whatever garment lay to hand. Old Clint touched a match to a lantern and started off toward the creek, his shadow wavering crazily on the snow.

The older boys followed him while Robin stood on the porch with Mother, straining his eyes and ears into the darkness.

Soon came the sound of the horses' hoofs, muffled by the snow, a lonely sound in the night. Then came the excited ring of the boys' voices, and the lantern light began to retrace its course. In a moment Robin could see the horses looming monstrous in the feeble light. Their heads drooped low.

Beside him Mother's voice rang out. "Are you all right, Bob?"

Father's voice came back, a croaking ghost of a voice. "Nothing wrong. Just done in."

The little cavalcade came up to the porch. Old Clint was leading Sheila by the bridle, and Father, slumped astride her, was a shapeless mass in his sheepskin coat. With a groan, he heaved himself out of the saddle. His knees gave way when he tried to stand and he seized the stirrup to keep from falling.

"Me and the boys'll see to the horses," Old Clint told him. "Go on in an' get yerself unfroze."

Father steadied himself on the railing as he climbed the steps. "That kitchen light," he said hoarsely, "I saw it five miles off. Most beautiful sight in the world."

"Robbie," said Mother, "put a kettle of water on the stove. We'll heat enough so Father can have a good hot bath."

Father slumped into a chair and let Mother help him off with his boots and coat. His face was nearly blue with cold and he talked as though it were a great effort to form the words with his lips.

Gradually the story came out. He had ridden hour after hour, mile after rugged mile, seeking out all the places he knew where sixty-odd head of cattle might have taken refuge from the storm. By three in the afternoon, already stiff with cold and weary to the bone, he was about to give up and head for home when the wind veered freakishly and brought him the sound of cattle bawling far to the south. In another half hour he found them. They were bunched in a semicircular canyon walled in on three sides by jagged rock—over which, Father said, nothing but a goat could climb—and on the fourth side by mountainous drifts of snow.

"You mean they can't get out?" put in Robin. Unlike Mother and Father he was not thinking of the great amount of money that sixty white-faced cattle represented. He was thinking only of the animals themselves, trapped by the snow and slowly dying of starvation.

"No, boy, they can't get out," said Father slowly. "But we've got one chance—if the weather will just give us a break." Robin's spirits soared.

While Father ate his supper he outlined his plan. "Everyone's going to have to pitch in," he began, "and it's going to mean an all-night job for some of us.

"Wynn, after I get through explaining, you ride up to the Alward place and tell them what I want. I'm sure Ed and his oldest boy will lend a hand. Clint, you'll be one to lose some sleep. I want you to take the wheels off the wagon and rig sled runners to it. Make sure the cat's warmed up and gassed and ready to go. Martha, I guess you'll have to lose sleep, too, because we're going to need food and plenty of it. I'm going to turn in as soon as I have that bath and I want you to roust me out about two in the morning.

"Now here's the program. We can't get the cattle out—at least not the way things are now—so we're going to haul feed in to them. It may

work and it may not but we've got to give it a try.
I figure the Denby place over by Coon Mountain
is a good ten miles closer to where the cattle are
than our own place is. With the cat, we can get
there by road, and maybe a ways farther on before the country gets too rough. The rest of the
way—maybe five-six miles—we'll have to use the
horses, the three that are harness-broke—Cotton
and Sheila and Fred, the new bay. The others
can be ridden on ahead to break trail. Soon as I
get up at two, Clint, you can turn in and get some
sleep. I'll load the hay—all the rig will carry—and
be ready to take off at daybreak. I'll pick up Alward at the head of his lane and the two of us
will go on to Denby's with the rig. . . . Wynn,
do you think you can handle Comet?"

"Sure, easy," replied Wynn, his bold eyes
gleaming in the lamplight.

"Just watch out he doesn't knock the cockiness
out of you," said Father dryly, "but you've got
to try. Barry, you ride another—not Sheila because she worked her heart out today and the
more rest she gets the better. The Alward boy can
take another. The rest you can lead. You'll start
about nine o'clock. Stick to the cat's trail and take

it easy, no cowboy stuff. You can pack the chow on the horses you lead. At Denby's—you ought to make it there about noon—give the horses a rest and grab a bite to eat. Then follow the trail we've made with the cat. If we bog down before you get there we'll build a fire and wait. Whatever you do, don't push those horses any harder than you have to."

Father paused and looked at the faces of the others, one by one. Then he said. "Now, everybody got his signals straight?"

Robin, staring at Father's plate, swallowed hard and said, "But what about me and—Magic?"

Barry, beside him, started a giggle that ended in a grunt, and Robin knew that Wynn had kicked him under the table.

"I haven't forgotten you, boy," said Father quickly, but Robin knew he had. "We can't leave Mother all alone, you know. Somebody's got to stay and look after her."

"Oh," said Robin. Then he added, though he knew it was no use, "But Clint will be here."

"No he won't," Father said. "He's going to take the wheel tractor and haul another load of feed to Denby's on the big trailer. And after that another load, if we get the first one through. So you see you've got to stay and look after Mother."

"All right," said Robin quietly.

There was an uncomfortable silence, broken suddenly by the same unearthly sound they had heard before dawn that morning—the scream of the cougar in the night. Old Mac came bristling to his feet and Father said, "That murdering devil's still around. Wish I had the time to go out after him."

"Folks better keep their stock under lock and key tonight," remarked Old Clint, shoving back his chair and getting stiffly to his feet. "Well, I best git on the job."

7

MAN OF THE HOUSE

ROBIN woke at dawn to the roar and clatter of the cat as it moved past the house and down the lane, but he lay dispiritedly in bed another hour, knowing that he had no part in the excitement of the day. Later he watched with admiration, and with envy too, while Wynn, using spurs and a quirt as well, fought the rebellious Comet to a standstill and started proudly down the lane at the head of his little cavalcade.

The temperature had risen steadily during the night, but it was still unseasonably cold and the sky was leaden with the threat of new snow. Magic, whom Robin had let out into the corral for a little exercise, watched the other horses until they were out of sight. Twice she nickered wistfully and Robin knew she felt out of things, just as he did.

To cheer them both he presented her with

an extra—and quite unnecessary—can of oats. "Maybe I couldn't do much," he told her, letting his hand slide lingeringly along her neck, "but you could, if they only knew it, and sometime we'll get a chance to show them all."

It was a comforting prophecy which Robin himself only half believed.

Between dinner and bedtime that night trouble came.

Robin was alone with Mother, for the wheeled tractor had refused to run, forcing Old Clint to make extensive repairs before starting out with his trailerload of hay. "Don't expect nobody back till late—mebbe till morning," were his last words to Mother. "Likely the boys'll bed down over to Denby's."

Mother, who had been up all the night before frying chicken, making sandwiches and coffee, was staggering with weariness. She insisted, though, on cleaning the kitchen to the last crumb, and Robin helped.

When they had finished, Mother said, "Now if you'll put a few more sticks of wood in the stove I'll take these crusts out for the birds and we'll be all done." In wintertime Mother never failed to scatter bits of food on the snow for the birds.

In the storeroom she tossed a coat around her shoulders and hurried out to the back porch. Robin was reaching for the wood box when he heard a scraping sound from the back steps, a thump, a startled cry from Mother, and then a

second thump which was louder than the first.

For a moment he stood frozen, his hands still outstretched toward the wood box. Then he ran to the back door and out. "Mother!" he called. "Mother, what's wrong?"

She lay at the bottom of the steps. Robin was at her side in an instant, bending over her, and then he saw that one of her legs was bent outward at an impossible angle. Her face was white as the snow itself.

Then she smiled with a visible effort and reached for his hand. This gesture steadied him.

She said, "It's all right, Robbie. You mustn't be excited. I did a very silly thing. I was tired and in a hurry and I didn't hold on to the rail. I slipped on the ice and fell."

"But Mother, your leg! It—it must be broken! What will we do?"

Mother closed her eyes a moment and her teeth were set together, and then she said, "We'll be calm, Robbie. We'll think about it and then we'll decide what to do. Now do you see why Father told you to stay with me?"

As she talked Robin felt suddenly ashamed of his fear. Strangely he thought too of Magic and the way he felt when he was on her back, as though her bigness and strength were his own. He said, "Mother, I'll take care of you. You'll be all right."

"Of course I will," she answered, and quickly Robin said, "First you've got to get in out of the cold. Does it hurt awfully?"

"No more than I can stand." And then, "Now remember this, Robin—whatever you do you mustn't strain yourself, because if you do you'll be sick. If you're sick I can't help you, and you can't help me. Do you see?"

"I see," said Robin, "and I'll be careful."

"All right then. I'm going to crawl up the steps and into the kitchen. You hold my leg as straight as you can, but you mustn't do any more than that. After we get inside we'll decide what else to do."

Doing his best to hold the injured leg out straight, Robin could not see Mother's face as she clawed her way from step to step, across the porch, through the little storeroom and into the blessed warmth of the kitchen.

Just inside the kitchen door, the end of her endurance came. Holding her knee as tenderly as if it were a baby, Robin was suddenly aware that she was no longer moving. She had fainted from pain and exertion.

For a moment panic threatened to return and Robin was tempted to scream at her to wake up. But he didn't. Instead he thought of Magic—it didn't even seem strange that he should think of her at a time like this—and he gently lowered the knee to the floor and stood up.

I can do what I have to do, he told himself firmly, but I won't have to do it alone, because I will have Magic to help me.

Then he went into Father's and Mother's room, taking care not to move too fast, and pulled the blankets off the bed. Returning, he laid them over Mother, turning her as far as he could to tuck the blankets under.

Going back again, he brought a pillow from the bed and was putting it under her head when she opened her eyes. He waited, straightening out her hair on the pillow, until she smiled the same white-lipped smile. She said, speaking through her teeth, "Thank you, Robbie, you're a good doctor. I'll be all right now until Clint comes back, or Father, or someone."

Robin took a deep breath and said, "I'm going to get somebody to help you."

"There's nobody to get," said Mother, not quite understanding. "They've all gone for the cattle. Remember?"

"I'm going to Alwards'," Robin said. "They'll get the doctor."

"But you can't! It's more than a mile. You mustn't try to go there by yourself!"

"I'm not going by myself," Robin said. "I'm going on Magic."

"Magic! Robin, she's too— You can't—" She struggled to raise herself up on one elbow, but Robin, a little surprised at his own firmness, gently pushed her down.

"I'm going, Mother," he said.

"Robin," she burst out, "I forbid it, do you hear?"

He looked down at her uncomfortably. "It doesn't sound right to say it, but there isn't— well, there isn't any way you can stop me. So I'm going."

He felt even more uncomfortable at the strange way she looked at him then and the glint of sudden tears in her eyes. After a moment she said softly, "I've got the stubbornest set of menfolks in the county."

Robin smiled with relief. "Before I go," he said, "is there anything else I can get for you?"

She thought a moment. "You might bring a glass of water—and some pills, in case my leg gets to hurting. They're in a little flat box in the medicine chest. Robin, I wish you'd be sensible and do as I say."

But he had already hurried off for the pills. Returning, he set the little box and a glass of water beside her, then went to the storeroom and put on all the clothing he could find—his boots, a sweater of his own and a sweater of Barry's, a scarf to wrap around his face and neck, and a woolen cap to cover his ears. Passing Father's gun cabinet he paused and, on an impulse he didn't stop to think about, reached in and took down a rifle. It was a .38 caliber repeating rifle and there was a clip of ammunition on a bracket. Robin took that too and shoved it into the magazine. Then he slung the rifle over his shoulder, military style, and marched toward the barn.

The golden mare still wore the blanket he had given her, and in it she looked lumpy and any-

thing but graceful. But Robin had no time to think of such things. He unlatched the heavy door and swung it open. Then he crossed the corral, slipping and sliding in the pits Magic's hoofs had made in the snow.

He tugged at the bars of the corral gate and slid them back as far as they needed to go. When he straightened up, his shoulder struck the outstretched nose of the golden mare, who had followed to see what he was up to. Robin spoke to her. "We're going for a ride, Magic, but you mustn't go too fast because I might get sick and I couldn't help Mother." He climbed the fence rail and clicked to her softly from the back of his throat. "Over here, Magic, move over here."

She quivered, then moved obediently toward the rail, and Robin slid to her back. Leaning down, he picked up the rifle where he had stood it against a post, and held it cradled in his arms. "Go now," he said, and squeezed his knees against her sides.

Magic hesitated, and began to walk, turning her head inquisitively right and left as though the world that lay beyond her stall and her corral were new and full of interesting things. It was a

long time since she had gone this way. Now and then she stumbled, caught herself and plodded on again, and each time Robin told her, "It's the snow, Magic. You aren't used to it and you've got to be careful."

DEATH FOR A KILLER

To ROBIN it seemed as though the ghostly road stretched on forever, as though the golden mare were walking along a gray-white cloud extending from the earth to the very heavens. Long before the track that Father's cat had made turned south to reveal suddenly the light that marked the Alward house, Robin's shoulders were shaking with cold. Once Magic swerved and pranced out of the track into the drifts beside it, peering off to the left where the ground rose abruptly toward the hills of the upland range. Startled, Robin spoke to her sharply, urging her back into the trail.

The Alward dogs announced Robin's coming. There were three of them but they seemed like a dozen when they charged out of the darkness to nip at Magic's heels. She ignored them, for she had known many dogs in her day and outlived most of them. Then there was a moving light inside the house and Mrs. Alward, big and fat and comfortable, was thrusting a lantern out the side door and saying, "Who's this? Robin—Robin Daveen! What on earth, child—is something wrong at home?"

And Robin was saying, with a kind of pride he'd never felt before, "Yes ma'am, it's Mother. She's broken her leg and I came to ask if you could help."

Fat Mrs. Alward did not hesitate a second. "Of course I can help, boy!"

Turning, she called into the house. "Joey, get your pony and ride over to the Baker place—fast. Tell Sam Baker Mrs. Daveen's hurt bad and he should go for the doctor. And mind you dress up good and warm. Hurry now!" To Robin she said, "Get down off that horse, boy, and come in. You must be near froze. I'll get my duds on and be ready to go to your place in a jiffy."

"How will you get there?" Robin asked. He couldn't picture Mrs. Alward's mountainous bulk seated on a horse.

"Walk!" she boomed. "Think I'm scairt of a

little exercise? Now you come on in here and warm up."

"Thank you," Robin answered, trying his best to be polite and nudging Magic at the same time with his left knee, "but I'd better get back."

"Don't be foolish," she said, taking a step toward him. Fearing she intended to lift him down bodily, Robin dug his heels into Magic's sides and she moved obediently forward. He called over his shoulder, untruthfully, "I'm warm enough and—and I'd better get back."

"Well, all right," her voice boomed after him doubtfully. "You tell your ma I'll be there quick as I can."

In a minute or two Magic rounded the bend in the road, and the light of the Alward house vanished. Robin was alone again in the immensity of white earth and black sky. There was no sound but the muffled clop of Magic's hoofs in the snow.

Robin clamped his jaws to keep his teeth from chattering and hugged the rifle against his chest as though there were warmth in it. He had been foolish to bring it along, he thought, because if it weren't for the rifle he could have lain full-length on Magic's back, taken a little warmth from her.

The golden mare plodded steadily on, needing no guiding hand now, for she was going home. Numbed by the cold, Robin gradually fell into a curious dreamlike state in which nothing seemed quite real, and when at last the grove of bare, black trees that marked the end of his home lane loomed up ahead, he scarcely noticed.

But even if he had been warm and alert he could not have been prepared for what happened next. Magic had turned and was heading up the lane when, with no hint of warning, she reared high in the air, twisting sideways and filling the night with a shuddering scream of terror. Robin was hurled to the ground with a jar that drove the breath from his lungs and set flashes of white light dancing in his head.

It was only a moment but it seemed forever before his head cleared and he could catch a breath of the biting air. The rifle, he noticed with surprise, was still clutched tight in his mittened hands. Ghostly huge in the dim light, Magic was plunging, snorting, and side-stepping in the middle of the road. He called to her sharply, "Magic! Steady now, steady!"

Even as he spoke, he caught a hint of movement among the shadowy trees. At the same instant, as though at a signal, sounding thin and faraway, came the high-pitched hunting cry of old Mac from inside the kitchen where Mother lay helpless. And in that instant the house with its warmth and safety seemed to move as far away from Robin as if it were on the moon, for he knew now what had frightened Magic, what had made the tiny ripple of movement among the trees.

Father's words sprang into his mind. "That murdering devil's still around." And Old Clint's. "Folks better keep their stock under lock and key tonight." Robin shivered now with a different kind of cold that knotted his stomach with fear and set his heart to pounding faster than it should. He felt the way he had felt in dreams when something monstrous was about to overtake him and he could not move to save himself. Only now it was no dream and there would be no comfort of waking up.

Then he called sharply, "Magic! Here, girl, here!"

And Magic came, driven by the same need that

made Robin call out to her—the need to be near the only familiar, friendly creature visible in a world of terror. She moved toward him slowly, her great body trembling, her silvery coat splotched with dark patches of sweat. The sound of her breathing was like thunder in the ominous stillness. Then she was standing above him and Robin felt his racing heart slow down a bit. He was not alone now. Knowing she had come to him for protection gave him the courage he desperately needed.

Slowly, as though he had done it hundreds of times, he raised himself to one knee, thrust the tip of his right-hand mitten into his mouth and pulled it off with his teeth.

The trigger was cold as ice when he curled his finger around it. The stubborn safety catch seemed to burn his thumb as he pressed it open.

Panic threatened to seize him again, for he felt a warning stab of pain. His heart had worked too hard already and he was going to be sick. He was going to drop face down in the snow, and the cougar, whose claws could tear the head from a sheep with a single blow, could do as he wished with Robin Daveen.

But still the rifle came up until the cold smoothness of its stock touched Robin's cheek and he peered along the dully glinting barrel into the shadows of the trees. The pain was coming stronger now, stabbing into his chest, and he wondered idly, as if it all were happening to somebody else, how long it would be before the blackness came and set him free.

Magic snorted and swung her head around toward the left, peering into the darkness at something Robin couldn't see. Automatically he turned with her, swinging the muzzle of the rifle with him. Then he saw it—a pair of yellow glowing eyes at the foot of the tree nearest the road. They glowed at the end of the rifle barrel like the headlights of an onrushing car, and then they were gone. Robin's finger tightened on the trigger and the gun roared out, splitting the night in two. The last thing he knew was the slam of its recoil against his shoulder. Then the pain trampled over him like stampeding cattle and he slumped down into the snow.

Half a mile down the road Mrs. Alward straightened to the crack of the rifle as though

the shot had been aimed at her, and she quickened her ungainly pace until her breath came in wheezing gasps. Ten minutes later she found Robin's limp form at the feet of the silvery horse who had rolled him over on his back, seeking comfort from him but warming him providentially with her breathing.

Mrs. Alward picked him up, not knowing that a hundred feet away, in among the trees, lay the body of a great tawny cat-of-the-mountains with a bullet in its brain. She carried Robin to the house and the golden mare followed, walking steady and calm, for her duty of the night was done.

Robin came back to the world a long time later —so long that the light of another day was pouring in the window. It was not his own window, but the big high window of the living room. He was on the sofa and he felt the drowsy weariness he always felt when the doctor had been there and given him something to take the pain away and make him sleep.

The next thing he saw was the kind, lumpy face of Mrs. Alward, who was looking down at him, her big hands on her hips. She smiled and tipped her head to one side and said, "Well, aren't you going to say howdy to your room-mate?"

He rolled his head over and looked into the smiling-sober eyes of Mother, who was lying on a couch beside him. She reached across the narrow space that separated them and took his hand in hers, holding it lightly. She said, "Hi, Robbie," and he thought her leg must hurt her very much, for tears came quickly to her eyes.

"Mother," he said, "are you all right? Is your leg—"

"The leg's all right," she answered. "The doctor fixed it up—and gave me a talking-to besides, for being so silly and careless."

Father came in then. He looked big and awkward and rough, for he hadn't shaved and the black beard darkened his jaws. In his face too was the weariness of a man who has spent the last of his strength.

Not until Father kneeled down by the sofa did Robin see the surprising brightness in his eyes too before he rubbed big knuckles across them angrily.

"Hello, Father," Robin said. Father's throat moved as though he were swallowing a very large bite. He waited a moment, cleared his throat violently and said, "Reckon you'd like a dandy lion-skin rug for your room, boy? With the head stuffed and everything?"

"You mean I hit him?" Robin asked.

"Right between the eyes!" Father said with enormous pride. "Neat a shot as I've ever seen." His voice grew louder. "Tell me how it happened, Robbie. I've been busting to know for hours."

But Mother spoke quietly from her couch. "Not now, Bob. Later."

"Sure, tell me later," said Father quickly.

A thought struck Robin and he looked at Father sharply. "Magic!" he burst out. "Is she—"

"She's in her stall right now," said Father, "busy eating three times the feed a horse should have. I figured she must have had something to do with it."

"She had a lot to do with it," Robin said, remembering. "She came to me. She was awfully afraid but she came to me and—"

"Later, Robin," put in Mother softly. "Tell it later."

Father stood up. "I'll get out of here now," he said, "and go crawl in bed. I'm dead for sleep. But I had to wait and tell you I gave you the toughest job of all and you did it like a man."

Then he was gone and Robin lay for a long time quietly, still seeing Father's face up near the ceiling. After that he thought of something he had forgotten. "Mother," he said, "did they get the hay in to the cattle?"

"They did," she answered, "and what's more they found a way to get them out. By nightfall they should be back safe and sound."

"I'm glad," sighed Robin. He was feeling terribly drowsy now. "I'm glad they won't have to be out there in the cold any more. It gets awfully cold out there at night."

CHAPTER

9

THE WHITE STALLION

LOOKING back on it, Robin always thought of the winter of the Big Snow as one of the finest times he had known. On the surface of things nothing was so very different after the night of the cougar. But all the same Robin could tell that things had changed.

Wynn, for example, took to calling him Robin Hood, and Father, when he went to town or on some other errand that would take him away from home for a few hours, would sometimes wink at Mother and say, "Well, I can stay away as long as I want. You're in good hands with old Dead-Eye here." Even Barry, though he said nothing positive, carefully refrained from boasting about what a marksman he would be if only he had the chance.

It was a memorable time, because of these things and because of the winter itself. Those first days of snow were not the last. The weather turned mild just long enough for Father and the others to drive the cattle home and settle them in the pasture, where they could be looked after properly. Then a new storm came, and another and another, burying the high country under a layer of snow deeper than any within memory.

But spring came at last, and summer, and a winter again, and another summer, and then it was October and autumn mists hovered in the valleys and Robin was twelve years old.

The days were bright and should have been joyful too. But Robin's mind was troubled and fearful. Perhaps being twelve was a part of it, he thought, and he didn't like growing older if it was going to make him see things in a new and frightening way.

For there were moments now and then—no matter how quickly he slammed the doors of his mind against them—when the beauty, the dainty step, and the prideful carriage of the golden mare would slip away from her. They were only the briefest moments and each time Robin was able to rid his mind of them quickly, but they left him more troubled than ever.

The White Stallion

It was on the brightest morning of all that Magic refused to get up from her straw bed and eat the food he brought her. She raised her head wearily and whispered in her throat, but that was all.

A minute later, pale with fright, Robin startled Father, who was working at his desk in the dining room. "It's Magic, Father, she's sick! You've got to do something. Hurry!"

At the barn Father knelt in the straw beside the golden mare and put his ear to her neck and listened while Robin stood watching. Then Father pushed back her eyelid and looked under it. After that he got up slowly as if he himself were tired and ill. Robin followed every move with his eyes, while Father seemed to look at everything around him but the face of his youngest son.

"What is it?" Robin burst out. "Can you tell? Is it something bad?"

Father's voice was gruff as if he were angry at something. "She's a sick horse, boy. I'll call Doc Fields." He hesitated, looking down at the golden mare, and added, "He'll do the best he can, Robbie, but there are some things not even a good vet can do much about."

Robin felt himself slowly turning to ice from the inside out, but Father spoke again, more briskly. "Tell you what you do. Go get Clint—he's cutting cornstalks for the cattle—and tell him I said to help you mix up a wet mash. Likely she'll eat that. He'll know what to do."

Robin started instantly for the cornfield. There was vast comfort in having something to do for Magic. "Mind you don't go too fast!" Father called after him, then strode toward the house.

In the kitchen he encountered Mother's anxious eyes and nodded. "The old girl's at the end of the trail," he said. "I'm going to call Doc Fields, but just for the boy's sake. There's not much Doc can do."

"Maybe," said Mother, "he can at least stave it off for a while."

Father shook his head and angrily jerked the phone from its hook on the wall. "That horse is getting mighty close to thirty years old. It's only the boy's care and love that's kept her going this long."

Doc Fields was a giant of a man with a laugh that rumbled like thunder and huge hands that could be as gentle as a girl's. Father met his battered old truck at the end of the lane.

"I've brought you out on a wild goose chase, Doc. There's nothing you can do for the old mare. But it's for the sake of the boy—my youngest. He's going to take it hard and we want to spare him as best we can."

The big man's face grew sober. "Whatever I can do, Bob. Got anything in mind?"

"I have," Father said, "if we can pull it off. You take a look at the horse, make noises like a vet, and then say it will be best if you take her to your place, where you can look after her better. That way we can break it to him gradually."

The veterinarian nodded emphatically and slammed the truck in gear. "I got it," he boomed. "Let's go."

It was a good plan but it came to nothing, because of Robin. When he heard Doc Fields's proposal his face grew suddenly so white that Father reached toward him in alarm. But Robin stepped away, evading him, and shouted, "You can't take her away! Without me she— No one can take care of her the way I can. I'll stay with her all the time, I'll do anything you say, I'll—"

The big man started to speak, but Father threw him a warning look and said, "All right, boy. If that's the way you want it we'll keep her here."

Doc Fields said hastily, "O.K., son, whatever you say. I'll do all I can right now and I'll be back tomorrow and have another look at her."

Supper that night was a gloomy time. Robin knew the others were casting frequent looks at him while pretending not to. He knew too that Wynn's gay talk and joking were meant to cheer him up, but they only added to the fear that was growing in him like a weed. Even Barry was subdued and ate only half as much as usual. Robin ate almost nothing and excused himself as soon as possible to go back to Magic's stall. There he heaped clean straw around her and sat beside her, stroking her neck and speaking words of encouragement until Father came and got him off to bed by promising to look in on Magic during the night.

When Father, true to his word, visited the stall it was nearly midnight. Old Clint was leaning against the door frame staring moodily down at the golden mare. "What the Sam Hill are you doing here?" Father asked. "Thought you went to bed hours ago."

"Couldn't sleep," said the old man curtly, not even looking around.

Father gave him a curious glance. It was a rare night when Old Clint was not in bed and snoring by nine o'clock. Then Father too looked down at Magic. After a moment he asked, "How's the old girl doing?"

"No better, no worse."

There was another silence while Father stared at the old man. He said, "You sure are a chatterbox tonight."

Clint appeared not even to have heard until he suddenly burst out, "Dad burn it! How'm I ever goin' to face the boy again?"

"What do you mean?" asked Father, puzzled.

"You know blame well what I mean! Told me yourself I better have a good story ready when it come time for this old horse to go. Well, I ain't got one."

Father thought a moment. "Oh, yes," he said. "I'd forgotten.

Once started, the words shot out of Old Clint like popping corks. "Somebody'd ought to have busted me over the head with a fence post 'fore I told him she'd live forever—and him standin' there trustin' and believin' me!"

Father's big hand gently gripped Clint's bony shoulder for a moment. "You only meant a kindness by it," he said. "Besides, he's probably forgotten—"

"No he ain't," the old man interrupted, "not for a minute he ain't. I know! Tonight at supper I sneaked a look at him and he was a-watchin' me, them big eyes scared-like but hopeful too, wantin' me to speak up, tell him I wasn't no liar and his horse wasn't goin' to die—wantin' me to say it but afeared to ask." He fumbled in his overalls and brought out his snuffbox with a shaking hand. "I near choked on my food."

Father sighed heavily and stepped inside the stall for a closer look at Magic. Over his shoulder he said, "It's a rough time for us all. But you're blaming yourself too much, Clint. Nothing you or anyone else could do or say to Robbie would make it any easier for him. Better hike on in now and get some sleep."

Old Clint was not the only one to whom sleep would not come that night. In his bed upstairs Robin heard the old man come in and shuffle off to his room. A little later came Father's heavier tread, a muffled thump as he removed his shoes in the kitchen, then the long familiar racket of the kitchen clock as Father wound it up. After that Father's bed creaked as he settled his weight into it, and then the house was silent.

Still Robin lay staring into the darkness. He had no way of knowing how long he turned and twisted in his bed, but at last he could stand it no longer. Perhaps if he could be with Magic where he could touch her, talk to her, then he might think of something, some miraculous thing he could do. Quietly he got out of bed and slipped into his clothes.

The moon was riding down the westward limits of the sky, and beneath Robin's feet the grass was crisp with frost. Even without the moon he could have found the gate, crossed the barnyard, ducked beneath the lower rail of the corral fence and swung open the door to the stall. He had done it all so many times before.

Magic nickered softly and raised her head from the deep bed of straw. A finger of moonlight came in with Robin and streaked her coat with silver fire. Her eyes were circles of soft shadow with crosses of light at the centers, like great star sapphires.

Robin dropped to his knees beside her and put down the blanket he had brought from his bed. With one arm around her neck he spoke softly. "I'm going to stay with you, because there's something I've got to do—something to help you." Then he crawled to the corner, under the overhanging manger, and spread his blanket out. Lying there rolled up in the blanket he stared at the crisscross slivers of moonlight that came in through the cracks in the door, and he thought as he had never thought before.

When the great idea came to him it was like a light in the darkness, brighter than the moon outside. His eyes grew wide with the wonder of it and his voice when he began to speak was breathless.

"There's a place, Magic," he began, "a wonderful, happy place that's not like anything you've ever seen. And nobody knows quite where it is, but we're going to find it—just you and I . . ."

It was the finest story he had ever thought about or told, because it had a kind of glory in it. It was a long story too, so long that Robin never knew when he came to the end of it.

The moonbeams slowly crept across the floor as the world rolled on, and when his voice was still at last the night was nearly gone.

The story told how Robin knelt beside the golden mare and with his hand beneath her chin gently urged her to her feet. It told how she snorted the dust of sleep from her nose and shook herself, how Robin climbed onto her back, hoisting himself by a handful of her silken mane.

"It's a long way, Magic, and we'd better go," he said then and nudged her with his knees.

The golden mare quivered and moved out through the door into full moonlight, stepping daintily and high, her ears pricked forward hunting the sounds of the night.

"This time," he whispered, "is different from all the other times, and you've got to go fast. You've got to go faster than you ever went before." He nudged her harder, and she moved faster, faster still, changing her gaits with never a jolt, until the chill wind sang in Robin's ears and turned them numb. The wind sang so shrilly indeed that Robin never could remember afterward just when it was that the sound of hoofbeats ceased and the frosty night grew still.

Yet on she galloped, steadily, tirelessly, silent as a snowflake on the wind, and the shadowed valleys fled behind her and the trees blurred smokily together.

Robin, clinging tight to his handful of silvery mane, could scarcely see for the watering of his eyes in the cold and rushing air, but he blinked them clear and turned his head to look backward and down.

What he saw did not surprise him, though it made him dizzy all the same. The house and barn were tiny white squares at the edge of another square that was the lower pasture. Nearer, but

still below and behind, was the upland range, a
vast and ghostly jumble of rocks and shadows
and twisted trees. Nearer still were the mountaintops, hooded and cloaked in their eternal
snows, while the moonlight set their slopes to
gleaming and winds mourned among their crags.

Gazing at their vastness brought the blur to
Robin's eyes again and for a long time he could
see nothing but vague shifting shapes and colors.
Then gradually a strange light was over everything and the moon was nowhere to be seen.

Robin let go with one hand to rub his eyes and
at that moment he felt the golden mare's long,
reaching stride pull in and shorten. The air no
longer whistled in his ears and the bite of October was gone.

Then his eyes were open and he looked around
in wonder. There was no sun in the sky and yet
there was sunlight everywhere, the soft, warm
sunlight of a summer evening. On every hand as
far as his eyes could reach, green as a tropic sea
beneath the light, lay grasslands, the vastness of
them unbroken and unmarred by roads or fence
or any sign of human presence.

Slowed now to a gentle, swinging lope as easy

to sit as the gait of a rocking horse, Magic was moving through the grass that rose to her knees or higher. Everywhere were patches of crimson clover, vetch with its purple flowers, and silver-bearded oats. But the golden mare paid no heed to the feast that lay around her. Her head was high, her nostrils flaring as she tested the wind. Now and then she broke her gait to dance a little with excitement and a low, whispering nicker trembled in her throat.

Suddenly she stopped, planting her hoofs and stiffening her legs as solidly as a horse of steel. Caught by surprise, Robin slid forward over the hump of her withers and wildly threw his arms around her neck to keep from falling. His hands could feel her trembling, and his ear, against her soft neck, could hear the thudding of her heart.

Scrambling back to his proper seat, he lifted his head to look where she was looking and the breath rushed into him with a sound that was like a sob.

Far off to the right upon the endless grassland came a vast herd of horses, running wild and free, the silvery manes among them glinting like whitecaps in the sunlight.

Beneath him the golden mare was trembling harder but Robin scarcely noticed, because he was trembling too. The great herd was bearing down upon them like a storm, but strangely their myriad hoofs made no more noise than the breeze among the grasses.

They were nearer now and he could make out among their masses every kind of horse he had ever seen or heard about—from shaggy little ponies to mighty Belgians, scrubby cobs to clean-lined purebreds—piebalds, palominos, duns and dapple grays, sorrels, chestnuts, bays and browns and blacks.

Suddenly—magically, it seemed to Robin—their ranks parted and from their midst, like a flaming arrow, burst the most magnificent, majestic horse that was ever dreamed about, even by Robin Daveen. He was a stallion, pure white from his fine-drawn nose to the tail he carried like a banner in the wind as he raced ahead of the herd. Tumbling from the mighty span of his neck, his mane swept the grass at his side.

Watching, Robin found that his throat was dusty dry, that his hands were clenching the soft hair of Magic's neck so tightly they ached. His

eyes would not leave the figure of the great white stallion.

Suddenly, with a motion as light and free as a bird in the air, the great horse wheeled and faced the oncoming horde. His neigh, like a bugle in the night, sent a shiver racing up Robin's back.

The effect of that clear, commanding note was as magical as the white stallion himself. Those thousands—perhaps millions—of racing, milling horses halted as abruptly as if they were a single horse. Some dropped their heads to crop the long grass, but most of them stood motionless, waiting, switching their tails from time to time and staring toward the golden mare with soft, incurious eyes.

Wheeling again, the white horse left them and trotted across the green expanse remaining between the herd and the stranger who was Magic. His gait was effortless as flowing water and as full of power, the muscles bunching at his shoulders, his head imperiously high.

As he came nearer, Robin's breath grew shorter in amazement at the size of him. He stood twenty hands high or more, and Robin wondered where or when his like had ever been seen on the earth.

A few yards off he stopped. A nicker rumbled

deep in his chest and Magic answered eagerly, every muscle trembling. But he was not satisfied. He bent his head and pawed the ground and began to circle, stepping sideways like a horse in the circus ring. And as he circled he moved in, each step bringing him closer, closer still, until, while Robin held his breath, he stretched out his massive neck and sniffed at Robin's jacket.

In the next instant he had reared full up, his great hoofs slashing the air above Robin's head, a cry of anger bubbling from his throat, his ears laid flat against his head, lips drawn back from gleaming teeth.

Coming down, his hoofs grazed the shoulder of the golden mare and in terror she plunged backward. Again the great white stallion reared and struck out with hoofs that glistened in the golden light, screaming his displeasure.

It was then that Magic turned and bolted, fleeing from his anger. And Robin fell, her mane torn from his grasp, his body twisting sideways, plunging down into the long, soft grass.

10

END AND BEGINNING

WYNN found Robin in the stall soon after daybreak, sleeping soundly with the clean straw heaped around him.

The bold eyes of the older boy softened as he looked down at his brother. Wynn was sixteen now and almost as big as Father. A glance at the golden mare brought a frown to his face and he swore softly as he listened to her breathing. It bubbled and heaved as though she had run a long way.

Then he knelt in the straw and gently wakened Robin. "Come on, Robbie, you better get back in the house before Mother finds out you slept here."

Robin, struggling up from the depths of sleep, opened startled eyes and looked at Wynn. Suddenly he remembered and cried out, "It was my fault! It was my fault he wouldn't let her come with the others. Because I was there and I had no right to be."

Wynn's eyes were staring wide. "Who, Robbie?"

But Robin scarcely knew he had spoken. "You should have seen him. You can't even imagine how beautiful he is!"

"Who do you mean, Robbie?"

"The stallion—the great white stallion!"

Wynn's voice was gentle. "Was it maybe a dream?"

"NO!" said Robin violently. "No, I was there! I took Magic out and we—" He stopped, his eyes troubled.

But Wynn, struggling to understand, spoke softly. "Tell me about it, Robbie." And Robin, who could feel his big brother's honesty and puzzlement and affection, poured out the story of the wonderful ride in the night.

He told it all, every detail of it, and when he had finished he looked up at Wynn with a wistful hope in his eyes, and a kind of defiance too, and said almost in a whisper, "Maybe—maybe she'll go tonight. Alone."

Wynn looked away and for a long time said

nothing, his black brows knit in a scowl. At last he murmured, as though his mind were on other things, "Maybe she will."

Later, after Doc Fields had come and given the golden mare an injection that seemed to help her, and Robin had coaxed her to eat a little, Wynn herded Barry off into the tractor shed and faced him with a look of determination. "You and I," he said, "are going to do a job tonight. It's for Robbie. And if you ever let go even a hint of it to him, I'm telling you now"—he bunched his fist under Barry's nose—"I'll knock your head off!"

Barry slapped the fist away and Wynn saw to his amazement that the younger boy's eyes, almost on a level with his own, were filled with angry tears. And Barry was saying, "Maybe you'd like to try it now! What's the matter with you? You think you're the only one that—"

Wynn, looking down, kicked at an iron bolt that lay on the floor. "I'm not very bright," he said, "or I'd have known."

"Forget it," said Barry. "Just tell me what to do."

Robin paid no heed to the comings and goings of his brothers that day, for he spent every moment he could with the golden mare. Nor did he notice that night at supper when Barry furtively dropped a tiny white pill into his milk. And later, after he had gone back to keep his watch in the stall, he didn't know that Father came and lifted his arm from around Magic's neck and picked him up and carried him to bed.

Neither did he know—though Barry could have told him—what woke him later, when the night was no longer young. But his eyes were open and the light from his window told him that the moon was high along its misty road. The land lay sleeping, it seemed—all but Robin and the coyote who cried from the westward hill.

Then—and Robin jerked upright, flung the covers back and sprang for the window—there came like a bugle in the night the eager neigh of a horse and the drum of hoofbeats on the frosty ground. Robin pressed his face against the cold glass and peered out, searching the distance. But the mists lay low upon the land and blurred the probing moonbeams. Was that a swiftly moving shadow, far down in the lower pasture, or wasn't it? Robin never could be sure. Then, as suddenly as it began, the ruffling drum of hoofs broke off and the night was still again.

For a long time Robin stayed at the window, his eyes searching the mists and shadows. At last the coyote sang again from the hill and Robin shivered with cold and stood up.

Crossing to his bed, he stopped abruptly, seized by the temptation to tiptoe into his brothers' room and make sure of what in his heart he really knew—that they were not in their beds. At once he was ashamed of the thought. It would be an unworthy and disloyal thing if his brothers had done all this out of love for him. And besides, if he didn't go into their room he never could be really sure. . . . There would always be room for the thought—the blissfully comforting thought —that perhaps after all things had really happened very much as they happened in the story.

Resolutely he crawled back under the covers and lay with his eyes closed tight, willing himself to sleep. And after a while a smile spread over his face and lingered there, for in his mind he was looking across an unending sea of grass beneath a summer sky where a golden mare roamed free among her kind, lifting her forefeet high and daintily, where a great white stallion led the way, his tail like a banner in the wind, and where no men would ever come.

It was Barry who brought the news in the morning that the golden mare was gone. Thundering up the porch steps and into the house, slamming doors behind him, he announced, "She's gone! The door was open, I looked everywhere, but she's just plain disappeared!"

"Don't be silly, boy," Father said, looking quickly at Robin and then away. "She can't have disappeared."

"Likely she just wandered off," put in Old Clint. He didn't sound very convincing and added nervously, "Got to see to mending them fences."

Father said, "I'll go have a look myself."

Spooning the cream around in his oatmeal and carefully looking at nobody, Robin said, "It won't be any use, Father. Magic's gone. I was awake in the night, and I heard her go."

He raised his eyes and caught Wynn in a scowl so fierce it would have been frightening if Robin hadn't known what lay behind it. And then the scowl grew blurred around the edges and Wynn's face disappeared altogether as hot tears filled Robin's eyes.

His own words echoed on in his head: Magic's gone. But there was another thing, he thought. The golden mare was gone, and it was a hard, bitter time, but he did not feel lost and abandoned and alone—as he might have felt once, not so very long ago. Magic was gone, it was true, but Robin Daveen would never feel alone again.